In a Dark, Dark Room

In a Dark, Dark Room

and Other Scary Stories

Retold by Alvin Schwartz
Illustrated by Dirk Zimmer

 HarperTrophy

A Division of HarperCollinsPublishers

In a Dark, Dark Room and Other Scary Stories
Text copyright © 1984 by Alvin Schwartz
Illustrations copyright © 1984 by Dirk Zimmer
All rights reserved. No part of this book may be
used or reproduced in any manner whatsoever without
written permission except in the case of brief quotations
embodied in critical articles and reviews. Printed in
the United States of America. For information address
HarperCollins Children's Books, a division of
HarperCollins Publishers, 10 East 53rd Street, New
York, NY 10022.

Library of Congress Cataloging-in-Publication Data
Schwartz, Alvin, date
   In a dark, dark room, and other scary stories.

   (An I can read book)
   Summary: Seven scary stories to tell at night in
front of a fire or in the dark, based on traditional
stories and folktales from various countries.
   1. Tales.   2. Horror tales.   3. Children's stories.
[1. Folklore.   2. Horror stories.   3. Ghosts—Fiction.
4. Short stories]   1. Zimmer, Dirk, ill.   II. Title.
III. Series
PZ8.1.S399In 1984   398.2'5   [E]   83-47699
ISBN 0-06-025271-5
ISBN 0-06-025274-X (lib. bdg.)
ISBN 0-06-444090-7 (pbk.)

First Harper Trophy edition, 1985.

To Calliope

Contents

Foreword 9

1. THE TEETH 10

2. IN THE GRAVEYARD 18

3. THE GREEN RIBBON 24

4. IN A DARK, DARK ROOM 34

5. THE NIGHT IT RAINED 42

6. THE PIRATE 50

7. THE GHOST OF JOHN 60

Where the Stories Come From 63

Foreword

Most of us like scary stories

because we *like* feeling scared.

When there is no real danger,

feeling scared is fun.

The best time for these stories

is at night—

in front of a fire or in the dark.

Tell them s-l-o-w-l-y

and quietly,

and everyone will have

a good time.

The Teeth

I was hurrying home in the dark

when I saw a man

walking toward me.

"Do you know what time it is?"

I asked.

The man lit a match

to look at his watch.

"It is eight o'clock," he said.

Then he grinned at me.

His teeth were three inches long!

When I saw them, I ran.

12

Soon I came to another man.

"Why are you running?"

the man asked.

"I just met a man

with teeth this long,"

I said.

"It scared me."

"My teeth are longer than that,"

said the man,

and he grinned at me.

When I saw his teeth, I ran.

14

Soon I came to another man.

"Why are you running?"

he asked me.

"I just saw a man

with teeth this long,"

I said.

"That's nothing," said the man.

"Did you ever see teeth *this* long?"

I took one look,

and I ran all the way home.

In the Graveyard

A woman in a graveyard sat.

Ooooh!

Very short and very fat.

Ooooh!

She saw three corpses carried in.

Ooooh!

Very tall and very thin.

Ooooh!

To the corpses, the woman said,

"Will I be like you

when I am dead?"

Ooooh!

20

To the woman, the corpses said,

"You will be like us

when you are dead."

Ooooh!

To the corpses, the woman said,

"AAAAAAAAAAAH!"

The Green Ribbon

Once there was a girl named Jenny.

She was like all the other girls,

except for one thing.

She always wore a green ribbon

around her neck.

There was a boy named Alfred
in her class.
Alfred liked Jenny,
and Jenny liked Alfred.

One day he asked her,

"Why do you wear that ribbon

all the time?"

"I cannot tell you," said Jenny.

But Alfred kept asking,

"Why *do* you wear it?"

And Jenny would say,

"It is not important."

Jenny and Alfred grew up
and fell in love.
One day they got married.

After their wedding,

Alfred said,

"Now that we are married,

you must tell me

about the green ribbon."

"You still must wait,"

said Jenny.

"I will tell you

when the right time comes."

Years passed.

Alfred and Jenny grew old.

One day Jenny became very sick.

30

The doctor told her

she was dying.

Jenny called Alfred to her side.

31

"Alfred," she said,

"now I can tell you

about the green ribbon.

Untie it,

and you will see

why I could not tell you before."

Slowly and carefully,

Alfred untied the ribbon,

and Jenny's head fell off.

In a Dark, Dark Room

In a dark, dark wood,

there was a dark, dark house.

35

And in that dark, dark house,

there was a dark, dark room.

And in that dark, dark room,

there was a dark, dark chest.

And in that dark, dark chest,
there was a dark, dark shelf.

And on that dark, dark shelf,

there was a dark, dark box.

And in that dark, dark box,

there was—

39

A GHOST!

The Night It Rained

It was late at night.

I was driving past the cemetery

when I saw a boy

standing in the rain.

"Do you want a ride home?"

I asked.

"Yes, please," he said.

"I live on Front Street,

next to the school."

I handed him my old sweater.

"It is cold tonight," I said,

"and you are wet.

You had better put this on."

After that, we did not talk.

When we stopped at his house,

I said,

"Keep the sweater.

I will get it tomorrow.

What is your name?"

"Jim," he said.

"Thanks for the ride."

I stopped for the sweater

the next day.

A woman came to the door.

"Is Jim at home?" I asked.

"I have come

to pick up my sweater."

She looked at me
in a strange way.
"It must have been another boy,"
she said.
"Jim is our son.
But he has been dead
for almost a year.
He is buried in the cemetery."
I told her how sorry I was,
and I left.
I did not know what to think.

The next morning

I went to the cemetery.

I wanted to see Jim's grave.

Lying across the grave

was my sweater.

The Pirate

Ruth was spending her vacation

with her cousin Susan.

"A pirate once lived in our house,"
Susan told Ruth.

"He died in the room
where you are staying.
His ghost is supposed
to haunt that room.
But we have never seen it."

"I don't believe in ghosts,"
said Ruth.

But the thought of a pirate

haunting her room

scared her a little.

Before she got into bed that night,

Ruth looked everywhere.

She looked under the bed

and under the rug,

in the closet

and in the

drawers,

behind the dresser

and behind the curtains,

and anywhere else a ghost might hide.

But she did not find a thing.

Ruth yawned and stretched

and got into bed.

She turned off the light

and snuggled under the covers.

"Just as I thought,"

she said to herself.

"There is no one in this room

but me."

Then a big voice said,

"And *ME!*"

The Ghost of John

Have you seen the ghost of John?

Long white bones

and the flesh all g-o-n-e?

Ooooooooh!

Wouldn't it be chilly

with no skin o-n?

WHERE THE STORIES COME FROM

"The Teeth" is based on a story from Surinam (Dutch Guiana) collected in the 1920s by Melville and Frances Herskovitz.

"In the Graveyard" is a short version of the traditional song "Old Woman All Skin and Bone."

"The Green Ribbon" is based on a European folk motif in which a red thread is worn around a person's neck. The thread marks the place where the head was cut off, then reattached.

"In a Dark, Dark Room" is known in England and America.

"The Night It Rained" is based on variants of the widespread folktale "The Ghostly Hitchhiker."

"The Pirate" is based on a reference in *A Dictionary of British Folk-Tales in the English Language* by Katharine M. Briggs, v. 3, p. 416.

"The Ghost of John" was collected by the compiler in 1979 from Lynette M. Lee, age 8, Stockton, California.

ABOUT THE AUTHOR

Alvin Schwartz compiled over two dozen books of folklore for young readers that explores everything from wordplay and humor to tales and legends of all kinds. His books include TOMFOOLERY: *Trickery and Foolery with Words;* A TWISTER OF TWISTS, A TANGLER OF TONGUES; FLAPDOODLE: *Pure Nonsense from American Folklore;* and I SAW YOU IN THE BATHTUB *and Other Folk Rhymes* (an I Can Read Book); his very popular collections of scary stories— SCARY STORIES TO TELL IN THE DARK; MORE SCARY STORIES TO TELL IN THE DARK; SCARY STORIES 3; and the I Can Read Book, GHOSTS!

ABOUT THE ILLUSTRATOR

Dirk Zimmer is a native of Germany who now lives in New York City. He attended the Academie of Fine Arts in Hamburg, Germany, and his work has been shown in private galleries in Switzerland, Germany, and France. Mr. Zimmer has illustrated several children's books, including one he wrote himself: THE TRICK-OR-TREAT TRAP.